Songs from Dreamland

Songs from Dreamland

Original Lullabies by Lois Duncan

Illustrated by Kay Chorao

ALFRED A. KNOPF • NEW YORK

THIS IS A BORZOI BOOK PUBLISHED BY ALFRED A. KNOPF, INC.

Text copyright © 1989 by Lois Duncan and Robin Arquette
Illustrations copyright © 1989 by Kay Chorao
All rights reserved under International and Pan-American Copyright Conventions. Published
in the United States by Alfred A. Knopf, Inc., New York, and simultaneously in Canada by
Random House of Canada Limited, Toronto. Distributed by Random House, Inc., New York.

Manufactured in the United States of America   Book design by Mina Greenstein
1   3   5   7   9   10   8   6   4   2

Library of Congress Cataloging-in-Publication Data
Duncan, Lois, 1934–. Songs from dreamland : original lullabies / by Lois Duncan.   p.   cm.
Summary: An illustrated collection of lullabies and poems about sleep.   ISBN 0-394-89904-0
(trade) ISBN 0-394-99904-5 (lib. bdg.) ISBN 0-394-82862-3 (book-cassette)   1. Lullabies,
American.   2. Sleep—Juvenile poetry.   3. Children's poetry, American.   [1. Lullabies.
2. Sleep—Poetry.   3. American poetry.]   I. Chorao, Kay, ill.   II. Title.
PS3554.U464S66   1989   811'.54—dc19   88-21742

For Erin and Brittany Mahrer with love
—L.D. and R.A.

For Janet Schulman
—K.C.

WIND SONG

Wind at the window, sing us a silver song,
Silver as foam on an icy sea—
Silver as snow light,
Piercing the winter night,
Wind song and snow song for baby and me.

Wind song, silver song for us—
Sing it for baby and me.

Moon in the meadow, croon us a golden song,
Gold as the hum of the drowsy bees—
Gold as the moonlight,
Flooding the summer night,
Bee song and moon song for baby and me.

Moon song, golden song for us—
Sing it for baby and me.

Gold songs, silver songs for us—
Sing them for baby and me.

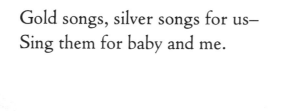

ROCKING CHAIR SONG

Somebody's baby is funny and fat—
Somebody's baby is naughty—
Somebody's baby got mad at the cat,
And somebody's baby is sorry for that.

Rock, rock–rock, rock–
Mother's rocking baby—
Rock, rock–rock, rock–
Mother's rocking baby.

Somebody's baby is bonny and bright—
Somebody's baby is funny—
Somebody's baby won't nap when it's light,
So somebody's baby gets cranky at night.

Rock, rock–rock, rock–
Mother's rocking baby—
Rock, rock–rock, rock–
Mother's rocking baby.

Somebody's baby is covered with crumbs—
Somebody's baby likes cookies—
Sooner or later the Sandman will come,
For somebody's baby is sucking a thumb.

Rock, rock–rock, rock–
Mother's rocking baby—
Rock, rock–rock, rock–
Mother's rocking baby.

WISH ON A STAR

Look out the window and wish on a star!
Wish on it quickly wherever you are.
Wish for the dream most important to you—
Wish, and that dream may come true.

Wish for a fuzzy warm kitten to hold.
Wish for a pony with hooves made of gold.
Wish for a necklace of sunbeams and dew—
Wish, and your dream may come true.

For the first star at night is a wondrous light
That is placed in the sky by the elves.
As it twinkles and gleams it can grant us our dreams,
As we know, for we've tried it ourselves—

Mommy and Daddy once wished on a star,
Wished on that magical light from afar,
Wished for a baby exactly like you—
See how our dream has come true!

THE SLEEPY SUN

When the sun is getting sleepy,
She slides down behind the trees,
Where she snuggles while she listens
To the singing of the breeze.
When my baby's getting sleepy,
He climbs up into my lap,
And he lets me sing him love songs
While he takes a little nap.

When the sun is very sleepy,
She slides down behind the hill,
Where she dozes in the shadows
While the world grows dark and still.
When my baby's very sleepy,
He leans back against my chest,
And he lets me hold and rock him
While he takes a little rest.

When the sun is *really* sleepy,
She slides down into the sea,
Where she dreams among the fishes
Of the day that's yet to be.
When my baby's *really* sleepy,
He falls fast asleep, and then,
He dreams of golden morning,
When the sun gets up again.

WHAT DID YOU DO TODAY?

What did you do today, little dog?
What did you do today?
"I went for a run on a rabbit trail.
I barked at the postman who brought the mail.
I yipped and I yapped, and I wagged my tail,
And that's what I did today."

Good night, little dog. Good night, little dog.
You have done everything right, little dog.
And now it is time to sleep tight, little dog,
For you've had a busy day.

What did you do today, little cat?
What did you do today?
"I purred so hard that my throat got sore.
I cleaned up a spill from the kitchen floor.
I got in a fight with the cat next door,
And that's what I did today."

Good night, little cat. Good night, little cat.
You have done everything right, little cat.
And now it is time to sleep tight, little cat,
For you've had a busy day.

What did you do today, little child?
What did you do today?
"I played in the car while we rode downtown.
I played in the park till the sun went down.
I played in the bath till the washrag drowned,
And that's what I did today."

Good night, little child. Good night, little child.
You have done everything right, little child.
Now I will snuggle you tight, little child,
For it's been a busy day.

TUCKING-IN SONG

Just one drink of water
Is all you will get.
With two drinks of water,
The bed might be wet.
With three drinks of water,
And one swallow more,
You'll find yourself swimming
Right out through the door.
So one drink of water—please, don't gulp that water—
One small cup of water, and not a drop more.

Just one bedtime story
Is all I will read.
For two bedtime stories
Are more than you need,
And three bedtime stories
Would take us all night;
We wouldn't be done
Till the sky filled with light.
So one bedtime story—one fairy-tale story—
One happy-end story, is all for tonight.

Just one good-night kiss
On the tip of your nose.
Then ten good-night kisses
On all of your toes.
A hundred more kisses
(That seems like so few),
There's just not enough
For a baby like you.
For kisses are different—and kisses are special—
And one good-night kiss—well, that just wouldn't do!

MOMMY'S TIRED TONIGHT

Baby, baby, loves to watch the moon,
Rising, rising, like a gold balloon.
Baby, baby, with your eyes so bright,
Close your eyes–close your eyes–
Mommy's tired tonight.

Baby, baby, loves the night bird's song,
Listens, listens, to it all night long.
Baby, baby, morning songs are best–
Go to sleep–go to sleep–
Mommy needs her rest.

Baby, baby, you've been changed and fed.
Baby, baby, see the pretty bed.
Hold your blankie, dream a happy dream–
If you don't go to sleep,
Mommy's going to scream.

Go to sleep–go to sleep–
Dream a happy dream.

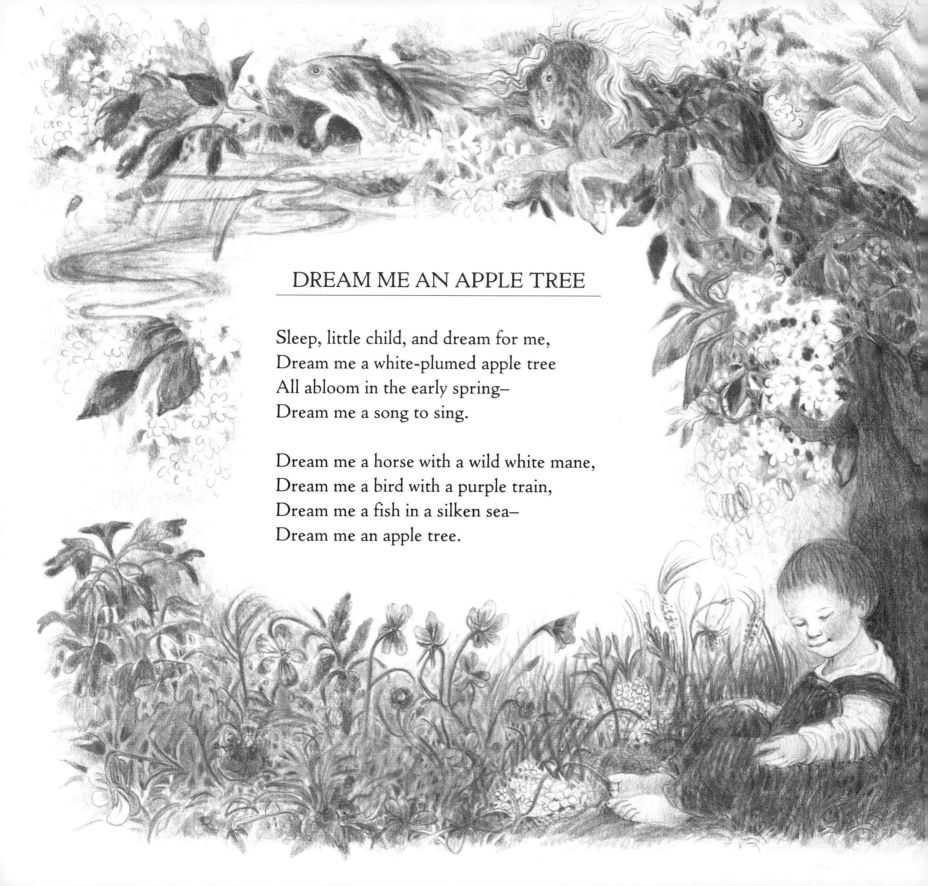

DREAM ME AN APPLE TREE

Sleep, little child, and dream for me,
Dream me a white-plumed apple tree
All abloom in the early spring–
Dream me a song to sing.

Dream me a horse with a wild white mane,
Dream me a bird with a purple train,
Dream me a fish in a silken sea–
Dream me an apple tree.

Fresh from a land where dreams are made,
Tired child rests in a tree's cool shade,
Blossoms float in a silver stream—
Dream me a springtime dream.

Sleep, little child, and dream for me,
Dream me a house in an apple tree,
White lace ceiling and grass-green floor—
Dream me a child once more.

RED BIRD

Bright red bird on the branch above,
Hush your squawks and your "Peep, peep, peep."
Sing a song for the child I love—
Then fold your wings and sleep.

Brown-tailed squirrel in the maple tree,
Chat, chat, chattered till darkness fell.
Off you go with a one, two, three—
Sleep well, brown squirrel, sleep well.

For I know a child who played today
A little too hard and long,
And I know a child worn out from play—
That's why I sing this song.

Tired little head against my breast,
Soft little arms that cling so tight,
Time has come now to get some rest—
Good night, my love, good night.

THE RAIN LADY

Soft in the darkness the Rain Lady comes,
Twirling her hair with the tips of her thumbs—
Hair that is sweet as a summertime dream,
Studded with raindrops that sparkle and gleam,
Hair that is gray as the mists of the sea,
Whirling and swirling and tumbling free—
Shush, shush, don't make a sound—
Rest while the rain comes down.

Soft in the darkness the Rain Lady stands,
Shaking her hair with her gentle white hands.
Chipmunks and rabbits and ferrets and moles,
Tiny wet field mice run into their holes,
Sheep on the hillside and lambs on the plain,
Little wool blotters that soak up the rain—
Shush, shush, don't make a sound—
Rest while the rain comes down.

Soft in the darkness the Rain Lady sings,
Voice that is cool as the winds of the spring.
Rain in the leaves makes a whispering sound,
Light as the silk of the Rain Lady's gown.
Rain on the roof makes a patter like drums.
Soft in the darkness the Rain Lady comes—
Shush, shush, don't make a sound—
Rest while the rain comes down.

SLEEPY TOWN

Close your eyes—settle down—
That's how we get to Sleepy Town.
Close your eyes—settle down—
That's how we get to Sleepy Town.

Think of the wind blowing far and free,
Teasing the waves as it skims the sea.

Think of a meadow where silken grass
Bows to the wind as it hurries past.

Think of the birds in the autumn sky,
Sailing like kites when the wind goes by.

Think of the wind in the trees above,
Calling the name of the child I love.

Close your eyes–settle down–
Ride with the wind to Sleepy Town.
Close your eyes–settle down–
Ride with the wind to Sleepy Town.

THE TRAINS TO DREAMLAND

The first train bound for Dreamland
Is revving up to go.
See the sleepy passengers
Standing in a row.
Some of them are tall and thin,
Some of them are stout,
And see the silly baby
With his jammies wrongside out.

The first train bound for Dreamland
Is chugging down the track—
Mama will be waiting
When the train comes back.

The second train to Dreamland
Is standing at the gate.
See the sleepy passengers
Helping load the freight—
Baby dolls to cuddle with,
Teddy bears to pet,
And lots of fuzzy blankets
With their corners sopping wet.

The second train to Dreamland
Is chugging down the track—
Mama will be waiting
When the train comes back.

The last train bound for Dreamland
Is getting set to start.
See the sleepy passengers
Ready to depart.
Some are from the Northern Lands,
Some are from the South,
And see the silly baby
With her fingers in her mouth.

The last train bound for Dreamland
Is chugging down the track—
Mama will be waiting
When the train comes back.

EVENING PRAYER

The beautiful day has slipped away,
And the night has moved gently in.
I kneel by my bed, and I offer thanks
For the wonderful time that has been,
For the song of the birds in the trees above
And the warmth of the golden sun.
I thank you, God, for your loving gift
Of the beautiful day that is done.

The beautiful night feels cool and right,
Now the warmth of the day is gone.
I kneel by my bed, and I offer thanks
For the wonderful hours till dawn,
For the crickets' song in the darkened hedge
While the stars fill the sky like flowers.
I thank you, God, for your loving gift
Of this beautiful night of ours.

SHIP IN THE NIGHT

Ship in the night–with salt in your sails–
Oh, what do you bring me from out of the deep?
"I bring you this wish from a magical fish–
Go to sleep. Go to sleep. Close your eyes. Go to sleep.
I bring you a comb that's frosted with foam,
A gift from a mermaid who wouldn't leave home,
And I'm bringing with me the song of the sea
To sing to the child that you love."

Ship in the night—with clouds in your sails—
Oh, what do you bring me from star-laden skies?
"A song that I heard from a magical bird—
Close your eyes. Close your eyes. Go to sleep. Close your eyes.
I've filled up my hold with gossamer gold
To weave you a blanket to keep out the cold,
And I bring you a tune I learned from the moon
To sing to the child that you love."

Lois Duncan, author of more than 30 novels for children and young adults, got the idea to write *Songs from Dreamland* when her first grandchild, Erin, who would not sleep at night, ran through the standard repertoire of "go-to-sleep" cassettes. Her eldest daughter, Robin Arquette, a professional singer and Erin's aunt, composed music to go with the lyrics. The lovely, lilting cassette *Songs from Dreamland* is the result of their collaboration.

Lois Duncan lives in Albuquerque, New Mexico, and Robin Arquette lives in Sarasota, Florida.

Kay Chorao is a fine painter who has written as well as illustrated many beautiful picture books. Her *The Baby's Lap Book, The Baby's Bedtime Book, The Baby's Good Morning Book,* and *The Baby's Storybook,* all of which are illustrated in a style similar to that of *Songs from Dreamland,* are considered outstanding books for the nursery-age child. She lives in New York City.